THE STORY THIEF

THE STORY THIEF

ANDREW FUSEK PETERS
ILLUSTRATED BY SARA UGOLOTTI

BLOOMSBURY EDUCATION
LONDON OXFORD NEW YORK NEW DELHI SYDNEY

BLOOMSBURY EDUCATION
Bloomsbury Publishing Plc
50 Bedford Square, London, WC1B 3DP, UK

BLOOMSBURY, BLOOMSBURY EDUCATION and the Diana logo
are trademarks of Bloomsbury Publishing Plc

First published in Great Britain in 2007 by A&C Black,
an imprint of Bloomsbury Publishing Plc

This edition published in 2020 by Bloomsbury Publishing Plc

Text copyright © Andrew Fusek Peters, 2007
IIllustrations copyright © Sara Ugolotti, 2020

Packaged for Bloomsbury by Plum5 Limited

Andrew Fusek Peters and Sara Ugolotti have asserted their rights under the Copyright,
Designs and Patents Act, 1988, to be identified as Author and Illustrator of this work

A catalogue record for this book is available from the British Library

ISBN: PB: 978-1-4729-7354-2;
ePDF: 978-1-4729-7355-9; ePub: 978-1-4729-7353-5

2 4 6 8 10 9 7 5 3 1

Printed and bound by CPI Group (UK) Ltd, Croydon, CR20 4YY

CONTENTS

CHAPTER ONE

Nyame the sky god lived in a huge room right on top of the clouds. He was the most bad-tempered god anyone had ever seen.

When Nyame had a tantrum,
everyone on Earth ran for cover.
When he complained,
the clouds
rumbled. When
he shouted,
thunder nearly
split people's
eardrums, sparks
flew from his eyes
as lightning, and

when his big, fat tears began to fall,
the land soon flooded.

Nyame had
one possession,
a treasure that
always cheered
him up. When
he opened
the big, brass
chest at the bottom of his bed, his
growls and grumbles stopped and
a smile like the sun lit up his face.
Because inside that chest was a bag.
And inside that bag were the words,
dreams and ideas that made up
every story ever told.

Nyame would pull out a story
and let its words soothe him to sleep.
If he was bored, nothing was better
than a good story. Stories helped
him pass the time, and filled his
empty dreams at night.

But what made him happiest was that every single one of the stories was his!

Down on Earth, people were bored. Their days were dull and their nights were long and silent as they sat round their fires. Why? Because there were no tales to tell, no one to fall in love with, no villains to outwit, no evil snakes to kill, no happy-ever-afters.

Anansi, the cleverest of spiders, scuttled across the land on her eight legs. Her silken webs hummed with the complaints of the people. Wherever she went, it was the same.

"If only we could have a good story to share!" said one.

"Our minds are as empty as calabash shells!" said another.

"With no ideas or dreams or tales, we are like rivers run dry," said a third.

Anansi decided that enough was enough. Although she could spin no yarn, she certainly *could* spin a web. So she did.

The web she span grew to make a ladder up into the sky. The wind tried to tear her threads, but she wove even harder. The clouds tried to move them away, but she held on tightly and wrapped them round with her sticky silk.

At last, she knocked on Nyame's door.

"Who is it?" the sky god boomed.

"Anansi, the cleverest of spiders!"

Nyame opened the door.

"And what does Anansi want with Nyame, the sky god who sees everything?"

Anansi crept into the room, hoping that the god wouldn't step on her and squash her flat.

"I've… I've come for your bag of stories," the spider stuttered.

"You have, have you?" Nyame roared. "And you think you can just walk in here and demand my most prized possession?"

"Yes!" Anansi puffed out her little chest and tried not to look terrified.

"Well, you are brave!" Nyame
stroked his beard and thought for
a moment.
"I tell you
what. If you
can bring me
Mmoboro,
the tribe of
hornets
whose stings
make you
swell like a

balloon; Osebo the leopard with
teeth like daggers; and Mmoatia,
the invisible fairy who dances where
nobody knows, then and only then
can you have my bag of stories!"

"Easy-peasy!" said Anansi.
"Not a problem. I'll see you
tomorrow then!"

Nyame burst out laughing as
the spider hopped and skipped out
of the room, and down her silvery
web. The tasks he had set were
impossible. That stupid spider didn't
stand a chance!

CHAPTER TWO

"It is impossible!" thought Anansi, as she landed back on Earth.

"How can a little spider like me capture a whole tribe of hornets?"

But as she crunched her favourite snack (dead, dried-up fly), an idea came to her.

"Of course! Now I know what to do!" she thought.

Anansi grabbed her knapsack and searched far and wide until she came to a coconut tree. With her eight legs, climbing the tree was no problem. She plucked a nice, ripe coconut and carried it back to the ground.

First she carved a hole in one end with her sharp teeth, then she drank the milk. Now all she needed was a plug. She found a cork tree and cut a plug that fitted the hole perfectly. Anansi took the coconut to the

nearest stream, filled it with water
and pushed in the cork.

Now it was time for action!
Anansi managed, with a lot of
huffing and puffing, to carry the
heavy coconut up the tree, where
the hornets had their hive. It was
midday, and the insects were having
a snooze as the hive swayed gently
at the end of a branch.

When Anansi was directly above the hive and hidden in the leaves, she pulled out the plug, took a deep breath and... poured the water on to the hornet's nest.

Within seconds, all the hornets flew out, buzzing angrily and ready to sting whoever had dared to attack them.

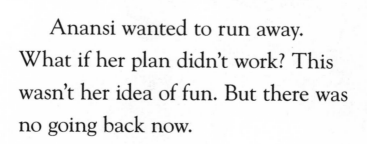

Anansi wanted to run away. What if her plan didn't work? This wasn't her idea of fun. But there was no going back now.

"Oh, great and graceful
Mmoboro, whose stings are as savage
as spears, I salute you," she said.

The queen hornet, who was
twice the size of the others, looked
up at the branches as she replied.

"Show yourself, invisible voice!
We are going to fill you with so
much poison that you burst!"

"But I have come to help!" said Anansi. "The rains have come and your hive is leaking!"

"That is true!" said the queen. "We were made wet. But why do you not show yourself? We do not know who you are and we do not trust you!"

Anansi parted the leaves.

"I am Anansi, the kindest of spiders!" she lied. "And my heart felt heavy when I thought you might lose your home."

The queen bowed. "It is good of you to think of us. Our hive is ruined and we are in trouble."

The queen believed her! Anansi couldn't believe her luck. Those hornets had stings bigger than their brains.

"Dear queen, I have a new home for you. Look!" Anansi pulled out the coconut. "The moment you fly in, I shall remove your old hive and weave a cradle for this new one!"

The queen was delighted. She turned to her tribe of hornets and commanded them to follow. Then, buzzing, they flew straight into the hole at the end of the coconut.

As the last hornet flew in, Anansi took out the plug and pushed it in.

"I've got you now!" she cried
with delight. "Anansi, the cleverest
of spiders, but not the most kind,
has captured Mmoboro, the tribe of
hornets whose stings make you swell
like a balloon!"

Then, with that, she tucked the buzzing coconut into her knapsack and set off to capture Osebo the leopard.

CHAPTER THREE

Osebo the leopard was bored.

He tried counting his spots, but there was a bit just behind his head that he couldn't see.

He flicked his tail at the endless, annoying flies, but they easily hovered out of the way.

He fancied playing a game, but all the local *game* had been eaten. By him. Most animals steered well clear of Osebo.

Except for Anansi, who walked straight up to the proud leopard.

"Good day to you, oh mighty-fanged Osebo!"

Osebo looked down at the little spider at his feet. "There's not much that's good about it. But thanks for the compliment, spider," he yawned, revealing a set of very sharp and bloodstained teeth.

Anansi shivered. This was far worse than the hornets.

"I wondered if you would like to play a game with me?"

"Play?" The leopard's ears shot up. "Play a game with you? What a dull idea! I can't think of anything less interesting to do…"

Osebo lifted one of his huge, padded paws to scratch behind his ear. "But it might be more fun than stamping on you, eh, spider?"

"Yes. Yes, of course," agreed Anansi, glad that her life had been spared.

The leopard rolled his eyes as if the whole thing was too much. But secretly he was very excited. "Go on then. What game shall we play? I'm all ears."

"Well…" Anansi tried to look like she was thinking deeply. Then suddenly her eyes lit up. "How about the tie-you-up game?"

"Never heard of it. Is it fun? I could do with a bit of fun."

"It's so funny, the tears will be rolling down your face, I promise!" said Anansi. "The game goes like this. I roll over and you tie me up. Then you untie me. You roll over and I tie you up. Then I untie you. Whoever makes the best knots wins the game!"

"Hmmm…" said Osebo, suspiciously. "It's a very strange kind of game."

"Trust me. Once we start and you get the hang of it, time will fly by!"

The leopard looked around. The sun sat still in the sky, blazing hotly. The flies buzzed around, doing their best to be annoying. It didn't sound like the most exciting game in the world, but it was better than doing nothing.

"All right then. I suppose I should start by tying up your eight skinny legs?" he said.

"Of course, oh lightning-limbed leopard!" agreed Anansi. "However, seeing as you're so clever and will obviously win, why don't we get my turn over and done with? You see, I'm not very good at tying knots…"

"Well, if you insist!" So Osebo the proud, but rather stupid, leopard rolled over and stuck his legs in the air. "Go on then. Show me how terrible your knots are!"

Now everyone, apart from Osebo that is, knows how good spiders are at weaving webs. Within seconds, Anansi had tied him up so tightly that the leopard was firmly trapped.

"Can you move your legs?" asked Anansi.

"No, not in the slightest. I have to say that I'm actually

quite impressed by your knots." Osebo smiled. "In fact, I think I'm beginning to enjoy this game. Right, my turn now. Untie me!"

"I didn't hear the magic word!" said Anansi. Osebo pouted.

"Untie me... please!"

"I'm afraid knot!" joked Anansi. "For, you see, the hunter has just been hunted!"

Osebo, the bound-up leopard, began to cry in shame. "You tricked me! It's not fair!" he wailed.

"But I didn't break my promise to you. Didn't I say that the tears would be rolling down your cheeks?"

Then, with that, Anansi pulled Osebo into her knapsack and set off to find Mmoatia, the invisible fairy who dances where nobody knows.

CHAPTER FOUR

Anansi's final task was the hardest.

"How am I going to find an invisible fairy? It's impossible!" she sighed. "Nyame has defeated me. I might as well give up."

But then she thought of all the miserable people who had no stories, and greedy, selfish Nyame, keeping this treasure all for himself.

Anansi sat down on her web and thought. And thought. And thought.

"That's it!" she cried.

A wise person had once told
her that fairies love to eat porridge,
especially if there is honey in it. And
with that fact in her head, the rest of
the plan was simple.

Anansi scuttled down to the river
and dug out a lump of clay.

With her eight legs, it was quick work to carve the soft material into the shape of a monkey's body. She took another lump and stuck it on a stick. This soon became a monkey's head, with the stick as a neck.

Then the spider raided her larder and found a big bottle of sticky molasses. She poured this over the monkey sculpture until it was covered from head to toe.

Finally, Anansi made a pot of porridge. She ate half of it, as all the work had made her hungry. She poured the other half into a bowl and drizzled some honey over the top. Then she placed the bowl in the monkey's lap.

Anansi hid behind the monkey's body, holding the stick with the head on it, and waited.

The scent of the porridge drifted away on the breeze. At last, it reached the nose of Mmoatia, the invisible fairy who dances where nobody knows.

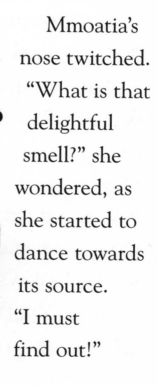

Mmoatia's nose twitched. "What is that delightful smell?" she wondered, as she started to dance towards its source. "I must find out!"

As she danced, her tummy began
to rumble so loudly that Anansi
heard and knew that the fairy was
on her way. When she reached the
monkey, the fairy stopped.

"Good day, monkey!" Behind the
monkey, Anansi tilted the stick.
The monkey bowed its head.

"May I share some of your porridge, please?" asked Mmoatia.

The monkey nodded its head. A spoon rose up in the air and a pair of invisible lips took a taste.

"This is delicious! Did you make it?"

The monkey nodded its head.

"May I have some more?"

The monkey nodded its head. The fairy tucked in and ate her fill. She wiped her lips and studied the monkey.

"What is your name, oh monkey who creates such wonderful feasts?"

This time, the monkey shook its head.

"Why don't you speak? It's rather rude, you know!"

The monkey shook its head. "Are you insulting me by not opening your mouth?" The fairy started to grow angry.

The monkey nodded its head. "How dare you not address me!"

The fairy lost her temper and struck the monkey on the shoulder. Her hand stuck fast. "What's this?

Let go of me, you brute!" She put her free hand on the monkey's other shoulder to try to pull herself away, but that hand stuck fast, too. She tried to kick the monkey, but her foot glued itself to its stomach. In seconds, the fairy was trapped.

"Greetings, Mmoatia, the
invisible fairy who dances where
nobody knows. Except me, that is!"
sang Anansi jumping out
from behind the
monkey.

"You tricked me! It's not fair!"
cried Mmoatia.

"No, I didn't! I simply gave you a nice meal and in return, you can do *me* a big favour!"

Then, with that, Anansi bundled the fairy into her knapsack, and set off to see Nyame the sky god.

CHAPTER FIVE

Anansi dragged her heavy knapsack
up the ladder into the clouds.
Puffing and panting, she
arrived at Nyame's door.

Knock! Knock! Knock!

"Go away!" thundered the
sky god.

"But I've brought you what you
asked for!" said Anansi.

"Impossible!" shouted Nyame,
opening the door. "Prove it!"

"Oh dear!" sighed Anansi.
"Well, you did ask!" She undid
the knapsack and poured out
its contents.

As the coconut rolled across the floor, the plug popped off and Mmoboro, the tribe of hornets, flew out. They were in a very bad mood indeed, especially since Anansi had told them it was Nyame who was to blame.

"Ooh! Oh! Ahhh!" screamed Nyame, hopping up and down in agony as the hornets stung him in revenge, before flying out of the open door and back down to their hive.

Osebo the leopard tumbled out next. Anansi was only too happy to untie the huge beast and let him loose.

Osebo took one look at Nyame and roared louder than any storm.

"Oh, please! Don't hurt me!" cried Nyame. He leaped onto his bed and ran round the room, trying to escape the leopard's sharp fangs. But Osebo pounced and brought the sky god crashing to the floor.

"Now, let me see!" said the leopard. "Shall I eat you? Or shall I not? I do so hate decisions."

"Please don't!" quivered the once-proud sky god.

"Well... you don't smell so good. And you're a little bit scrawny for my liking, so I suppose I'll let you go!"

"Oh, thank you! Nice pussy cat!" whimpered Nyame.

"Mind you, if you call me a pussy cat again, I might have to rip your head off," said Osebo.

"No. No. You are far greater than a pussy cat, oh prince of purr-fection!" said Nyame, desperate to be free.

"That's better!" said Osebo. He flicked his tail in Nyame's face and stalked off to the door, took one look down and jumped. Anansi's web made the perfect slide.

"Wheeeee!" shouted Osebo, as he tumbled back to Earth. He had finally found a game he enjoyed.

"There was one more thing you asked for, Nyame!" Anansi tipped up the knapsack and out came Mmoatia.

"My, you are a handsome sky god!" said the fairy. "Would you like a dance?"

Before Nyame could answer, something invisible grabbed both of his hands and danced him right out of his room.

And to this day, they are still dancing, which is why the sky never looks the same and the clouds are always moving.

Anansi smiled. She wove a slippery web onto the floor and slid the big brass chest over it towards the door. Then she gave it one, huge shove.

The chest fell through the clouds and landed with a crash on Earth, smashing into tiny pieces.

Stories of every colour, shape and size spilled out across the land; scary and sad, happy and hilarious; tales with twists and maidens with twisty hair; dragons and devils; angels and all sorts of heroes and heroines, with every ending under the sun.

They fluttered away and spread like seedlings. The people had been given the best gift of all and were never bored again.

Thanks to Anansi, the cleverest of spiders, every story ever told, every story ever written down, every story came from that chest, even this one!

READING ZONE!

WHAT DO YOU THINK?

Do you believe this story is the basis for all stories in the world?

What sort of story is it?

Do you think Anansi was brave or foolish?

Can you think of other stories where the smallest, most fragile character is the hero and stands up to other more powerful beings?

READING ZONE!

QUIZ TIME

Can you remember the answers
to these questions?

- Who was the most bad-tempered
  god anyone had ever seen?

- Why were the people on Earth
  so bored?

- How did Anansi trick the hornets
  so she could capture them?

- What did Anansi use to make the
  model of the monkey?

- What reasons does does
  Osebo give for not
  eating Nyame?